D IS For Dreidel

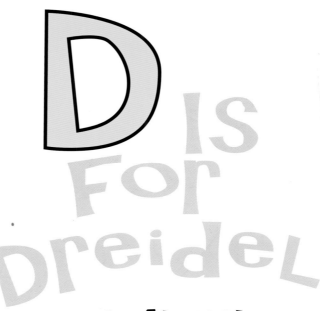

A Hanukkah Alphabet Book

For Liza and Jake, who are the light I celebrate every day of the year–T.L.S.

With thanks to Rabbi Alvin Wainhaus for his thoughtful review.

Text copyright © 2002 by Tanya Lee Stone. Illustrations copyright © 2002 by Dawn Apperley.
Published by Price Stern Sloan, a division of Penguin Putnam Books for Young Readers,
345 Hudson Street, New York, NY 10014. PSS! is a registered trademark of Penguin Putnam Inc.
Published simultaneously in Canada. Manufactured in China.

ISBN 0-8431-4576-5   C D E F G H I J

D IS For Dreidel

A HaNuKKaH ALPHabet BooK

By TaNya Lee StoNe

ILLUStrated by DaWN APPerLey

PSS!

PRICE STERN SLOAN

A is for afternoon

Sundown is near
Hanukkah's starting
The family's all here!

B is for bracha
The blessing we sing
And creamy cheese blintzes
Aunt Sarah will bring!

C is for challah bread
Braided in three
Pull off a hunk
And pass it to me!

D is for dreidel

Just twist it and spin
If it stops on gimel
Shout 'hooray', you win!

E is for **eight** days
Of Hanukkah joy
With treats and small presents
For each girl and boy!

F is for festival

Songs fill the air
The kids all play games
And bake cookies to share!

G is for gelt

The chocolatey kind
Peel back gold foil,
A treasure to find!

H is for hora

Join hands, dance around
The circle turns faster
It makes my heart pound!

I is for Israel

With its six-pointed star
It's our Jewish homeland
Wherever we are!

J is for Judah

A brave Maccabee
He fought with his brothers
To make the Jews free!

K is for kugel
A sweet noodle treat
My Grammy adds raisins
A great dish to eat!

L is for latkes
Crisp, chewy, and hot
Grate up some potatoes
We'll sure eat a lot!

M is for menorah
The symbol of light
It holds all the candles
They're lit left to right!

N is for neighborhood
So cheery at night
Menorahs in windows
Are shining their light!

O is for oil
It lasted eight days
A miracle light
That continued to blaze!

P is for presents
There's one for each night
Mom gave me a sweater
It's striped blue and white!

Q is for quilt

Wrapped around me so snug
My aunt made it for me
I gave her a hug!

R is for rabbi
Who leads us in prayer
Tells Hanukkah stories
And guides us with care!

S is for Shamash
The first candle lit
We light all the other
Bright candles with it!

T is for tzedakah

Perform a good deed
It's charity and giving
We help those in need!

Dreidel, Dreidel, Dreidel,
I made it out of clay

U is for uncles
All six come to stay
They laugh and tell jokes
And know fun games to play

V is for voices
Come follow along
Let's all sing the words to
The great dreidel song!

W is for winter
White blanket of snow
Sledding with cousins
And snowballs we throw!

X is for **xylophone**
Please play me a song
I gave one to Leah
She chimes all day long!

Y is for yarmulke

A cap for my head
To show true respect for
The prayers that I've said!

Z is for **Zaydee**
My grandpa's here, too
Our family sends wishes—
Happy Hanukkah to you!